Elephants never forget!

Anushka Ravishankar

Christiane Pieper

TARA PUBLISHING

It was quiet in the jungle... When a sudden storm came

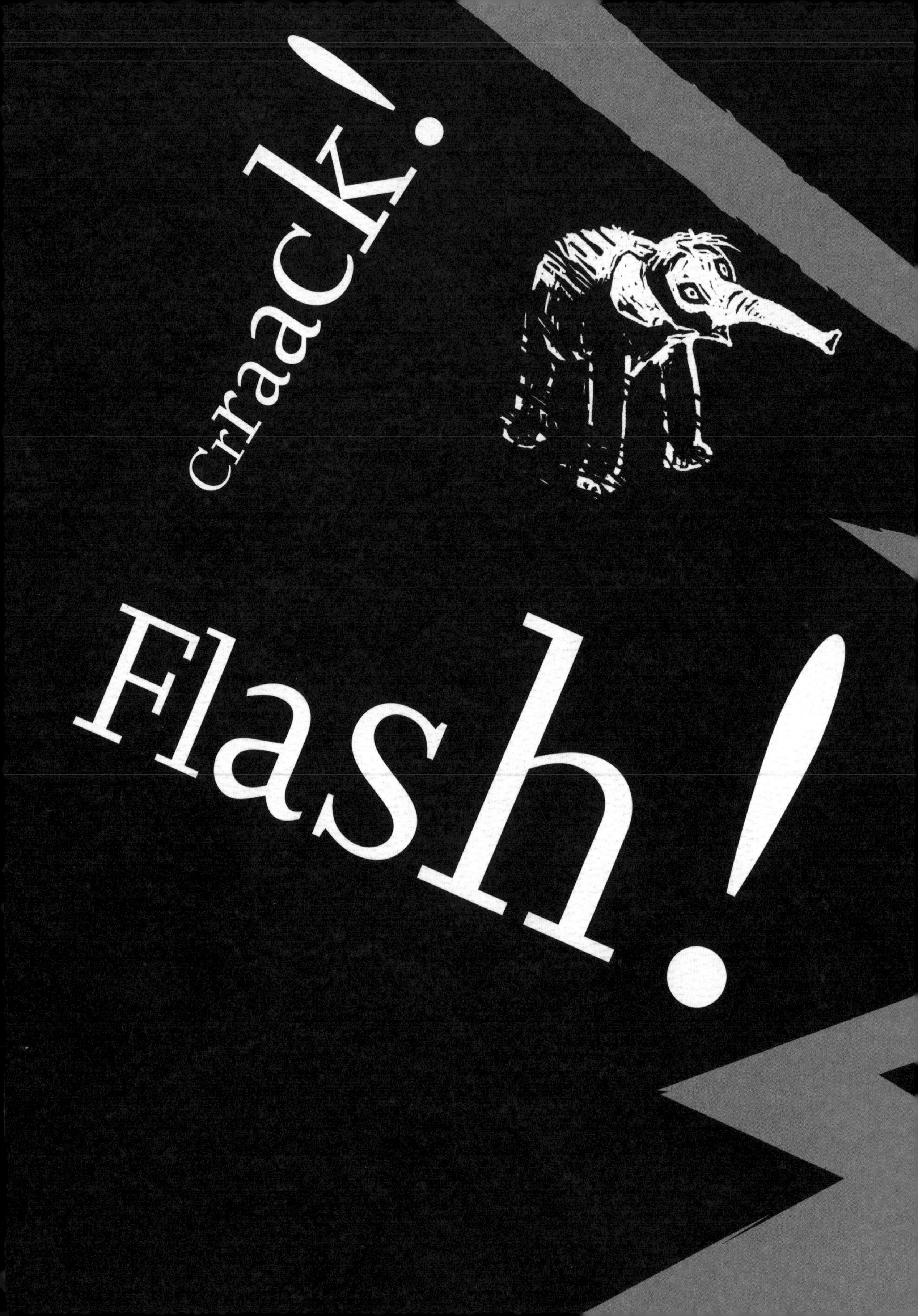
Crack!
Flash!

BOOM!

There was thunder, lightning, rain!

TOOT! TOOT!
The elephant
Trumpeted in fright.

HOOT! HOOT! HOOT!

The wind replied.

When it stopped raining
And the sun shone

The elephant found

He was all alone.

Splatter!

Splitter!

Chitter!

Chatter!

He heard a bunch of monkeys natter.

CCrrraCk!
A coconut hit him on his head

Enough, thought the elephant
And he fled.

He needed some water
To wash himself clean.

The buffaloes looked so calm, serene

The water was lovely, cool and green.

The elephant thought
He could stay with them

Maybe even play with them?

With a baby buffalo
He tumbled and wallowed

BELLOW!

The buffalo led
And the elephant followed

The elephant felt he had found a friend.

Their frolicking came to an end.

They were running away
The elephant was sad.

Why didn't they like him?
Was he smelly? Was he bad?

RA!

The reason they'd run
Was suddenly clear...

The elephant trembled in fear.

BELLLLOOOO

A buffalo pushed him aside.

As they ran away, they took him along

He stayed on with them
He grew big and strong.

The elephant cleared the buffaloes' path

He helped them have a shower bath

He found them leaves when the grass was dry

Now the tiger dared not come by.

His ears were too large
His nose was too long

His shape was quite odd
And his colour all wrong

He only could trumpet, he could not bellow
Yet, the elephant liked being a buffalo.

As they lazily wallowed in the river one day …

Some thirsty elephants
Came that way

The buffaloes decided
They'd rather not stay.

TOOooT! TOOo

T!

TOOooT!

The elephants called

Belloow! Belloooow!

The buffaloes bawled

Here?

      Or there?

Where should he go?

An elephant?

      Or a buffalo?

But in the end, the answer was plain-

A buffalo he would always remain!